AgriKids makes it fun for children to learn about farm safety and discover all there is to love about rural life.

To learn more about our products and what we do, visit AgriKids.ie.

For all the Delanys of Ashgrove, whose unwavering encouragement and enthusiasm has given me both inspiration and momentum! (They also have a red tractor!)

TALES FROM RIVERSIDE FARM

THE RED TRACTOR

ALMA JORDAN
ILLUSTRATED BY
MARTIN BECKETT

AgriKids
BE FARM SAFE
STAY FARM
SAFE

First published in 2015 by
AgriKids
Ashbawn, Corbal-lis
Julianstown, Co. Meath
www.agrikids.ie

Paperback	ISBN: 978 1 911013 167
eBook – mobi format	ISBN: 978 1 911013 174
eBook – ePub format	ISBN: 978 1 911013 181
CreateSpace edition	ISBN: 978 1 911013 198

Produced by Kazoo Independent Publishing Services
222 Beech Park, Lucan, Co. Dublin
www.kazoopublishing.com

Kazoo Independent Publishing Services is not the publisher of this work. All rights and responsibilities pertaining to this work remain with AgriKids.

Kazoo offers independent authors a full range of publishing services.
For further details visit www.kazoopublishing.com

Cover design by Andrew Brown
Cover and internal illustrations © Martin Beckett, One Tree Studio Ltd
Printed in the EU

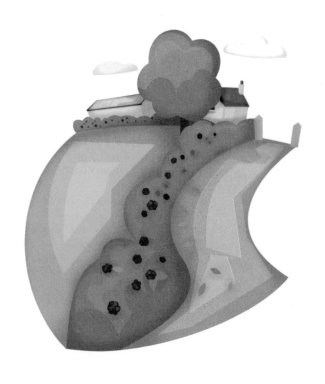

It was autumn on Riverside Farm. The leaves were turning brown, and the days were getting shorter.

All the apples, pears and blackberries were ready to be picked and baked into tasty tarts. MMM, autumn is a YUMMY time of year!

Tom and Sarah were outside playing football with Meg the sheepdog.

At least they were TRYING to play football, but Meg kept running away with the ball.

'COME BACK, MEG!' called Sarah.

Meg CHARGED around the corner with the ball in her mouth, and Tom and Sarah ran after her.

Meg was so EXCITED she ran straight into Mammy, who was carrying an ENORMOUS basket of washing.

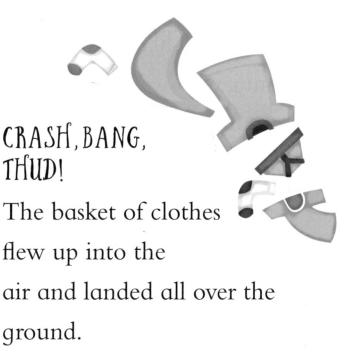

CRASH, BANG, THUD!

The basket of clothes
flew up into the
air and landed all over the
ground.

Meg had **KNOCKED** over poor
Mammy, who was sitting on
the ground with a pair of
Tom's **TRACTOR** socks
on her head.

'Is there something else you two can do while I hang out the washing?' said Mammy.

Tom and Sarah couldn't stop GIGGLING. Mammy looked so FUNNY with Tom's socks on her head.

After Tom and Sarah helped
pick up all the clothes,
Mammy handed them each a
bucket.

'There are lots and lots of BLACKBERRIES on the bushes. I want you to fill your BUCKETS with as many as you can. We can make BLACKBERRY TARTS later,' said Mammy.

Tom and Sarah LOVED
blackberry tarts.

'Remember,' said Mammy.
'Only pick the BLACK ones.
The RED ones will give us all a
tummy ache.'

The children grabbed their SCOOTERS and headed for the blackberry bushes. Maybe they would see their friend MR BRAMBLES, the hedge sprite.

'DUM DE DUM DE DIDDLY DO,'
sang Mr Brambles.

Autumn was a very BUSY time
for HEDGE SPRITES.

He had to ripen all the berries
and turn the leaves
from green to

brown.

Using his magic TWIG and a
BLACKBIRD'S feather, he TIPPED
and TAPPED and ZIPPED and
ZAPPED the berries
until they were
black, shiny and
very, very juicy.

'The birds and animals will have lots to eat over the winter,' he said. 'And there will be PLENTY left over for Mrs Brambles and me to make some blackberry jam. YUM!'

'WOW!' said Tom when he saw the bushes. 'There must be a MILLION blackberries here.'

'More like two million,' said Sarah. Her tummy was RUMBLING as she thought about BLACKBERRY TARTS.

'I hope our buckets will be big enough,' said Tom.

The children found the spot that had the most berries. It was right beside the gate to the back field.

'MR BRAMBLES, are you there?' called Tom and Sarah.

'OVER HERE, children,' said their little friend. 'Are you coming to pick some of my blackberries?'

 'We sure are,' said Tom as he reached for a berry.

'NO, Tom,' said Mr Brambles, 'that one is still too red.'

Mr Brambles flew up and
TAPPED the berry with his
feather. It immediately turned
into the blackest,
SHINIEST BERRY
the children
had ever
seen.

'MMM, thank
you, Mr Brambles,'
said Tom as he GOBBLED it up.

The sound of Daddy's RED TRACTOR made them all look up. Daddy and Jack were on their way to the back field.

'UH OH, grown-ups!' said Mr Brambles.

Hedge sprites don't like GROWN-UPS. They aren't any fun and they DON'T believe in magic. Can you IMAGINE that! NOT believing in magic!

'I must be OFF!' said Mr Brambles. 'The apples in the orchard need some of my MAGIC. Have fun, you two.'

And with that, he disappeared.

Daddy and Jack had
IMPORTANT work to do too.
The fence in the field needed
to be mended. Some of the
wood was
BROKEN, and
there were
holes big enough
for a sheep to
WRIGGLE through and get lost.

Everything Daddy and Jack needed was in the front bucket of the red tractor.

They had wire, nails, a big sledgehammer and wooden posts.

Daddy drove the RED TRACTOR up the hill to the top of the field. He turned off the engine and Jack hopped out.

'Don't forget the HANDBRAKE,' said Jack. 'We don't want the tractor to ROLL DOWN the hill.'

Daddy pulled
hard on the
handbrake until
it made a CLICK
sound.

Tom and
Sarah WAVED to
Daddy and Jack and
then set to work filling their
buckets – and their BELLIES!

Soon Daddy and Jack had
finished mending the fence on
one side of the field.

'We'll be done in no time,'
said Daddy as they drove the
tractor to the other side.

Jack hopped out. 'Don't forget
the HANDBRAKE!' he said again.

'I won't,' said Daddy. CLICK
went the
handbrake.

After a while, Tom got BORED
of picking blackberries. He
thought Daddy and Jack were
having more FUN.

'Can I sit in the red tractor and watch you fix the fence?' he asked Daddy.

'OK,' said Daddy, 'but DON'T touch anything.'

Tom climbed into the  red tractor and looked at all the buttons and lights.

'I wonder what this does?' he
said, holding a big black lever
with a button at the end of it.
Tom pressed the button –
CLICK! – and the
lever went
down.

With a loud GROAN, the red tractor started to roll DOWN the hill.

'THE TRACTOR!' shouted Jack. 'Tom must have let off the handbrake.'

'HELP!' cried Tom. 'What do I do?'

The red tractor picked up speed. Soon it was going too FAST for Daddy and Jack to catch it. FASTER and FASTER it went, heading straight for the bushes where Sarah was still picking blackberries.

'SARAH!' shouted Daddy.

Sarah LOOKED UP, her face covered in blackberry juice. She gasped in HORROR as she saw the tractor ZOOMING down the hill.

Daddy and Jack were RUNNING behind, waving their arms in the air. The wooden posts and tools were SCATTERED all over the field.

Tom CLUNG on to the seat as the tractor rolled over BUMPS and through holes. He was sure to crash and he was very FRIGHTENED.

Sarah knew only one person could help them now – MR BRAMBLES!

She remembered what their hedge sprite friend had told them the first time they met: 'Should you ever be in FEAR, call THREE TIMES and I will HEAR.'

'Mr Brambles, Mr Brambles, Mr Brambles,' cried Sarah.

SUDDENLY, she saw a ball of light fly into the red tractor, which was getting CLOSER and CLOSER to the blackberry bushes.

'SARAH!' cried Daddy again. The tractor was just a FEW METRES away from Sarah when it turned SHARPLY. Now it was heading STRAIGHT towards the field gate.

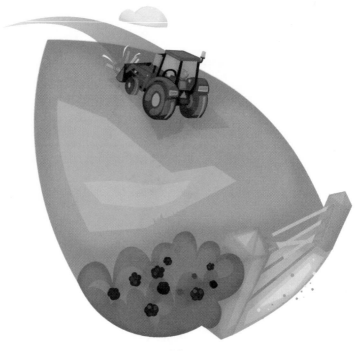

Jack couldn't BELIEVE his eyes. 'WHO is driving the tractor?' he cried.

'It MUST be Tom,' said Daddy.

The red tractor was about to
CRASH through the gate when,
as if by MAGIC, the gate SWUNG
open. The tractor ROLLED into
the farmyard and came to a
GENTLE stop in
front of the
big shed.

'How did the GATE open?' cried Jack.

'The wind must have BLOWN it open,' said Daddy.

Daddy and Jack RAN all the way to the farmyard.

'Tom, I told you NOT to touch anything,' said Daddy. 'I didn't know you could STEER a tractor.'

Tom said nothing. He HADN'T steered the tractor at all. It was Mr Brambles' MAGIC, but he would keep that a SECRET.

Daddy lifted Tom down and then went to help Jack pick up the wooden posts and tools.

As soon as Daddy was out of sight, Mr Brambles appeared again. 'PHEW! That was close,' he said. 'You two could have been BADLY hurt.'

'But we're OK thanks to you,' whispered Sarah.

'From now on, only play with TOY tractors, NOT real ones,' said Mr Brambles. 'Goodbye, children. Stay safe!'

'We will. Goodbye, Mr Brambles!' said Tom.

The children picked up their BUCKETS and headed back to the farmhouse with all the JUICY blackberries they had picked.

Later that day, something
made Mr Brambles' nose
TINGLE.

'What is that
DELICIOUS
smell?' he said.

He peeped through the branches of his hedge house and spotted a big BLACKBERRY TART. It was golden on the outside and full of YUMMY blackberries.

Beside the tart was a little card. It had a picture of Mr Brambles, Tom, Sarah and Meg on the front, and inside were the words THANK YOU!

'What a LOVELY card!' said Mr Brambles. 'I'm very LUCKY to have such good friends.'

Mr Brambles picked up the tart and FLEW to the farmyard to eat his TREAT in the autumn sun.

Jack was in the farmyard too.
He was checking the RED
TRACTOR to make
sure nothing
was BROKEN.

He still didn't understand
how the tractor had changed
direction. And how did the
gate OPEN all by itself?

'Something FUNNY is going on around here,' said Jack.

'First I saw a FLYING BULL, and now a tractor that can DRIVE itself.

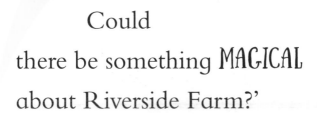

Could there be something MAGICAL about Riverside Farm?'

He shook his head and began to CHUCKLE. 'Don't be SILLY,' he said to himself. 'There's no such thing as MAGIC!'

Mr Brambles was sitting on the roof of the red tractor, MUNCHING happily on his blackberry tart. 'It's MAGIC all right,' he said with a grin. 'HEDGE SPRITE MAGIC!'

TALES FROM RIVERSIDE FARM
A New Way to Teach
Farm Safety to Children

ALSO AVAILABLE IN THE SERIES

For details on where to buy, visit
www.AgriKids.ie